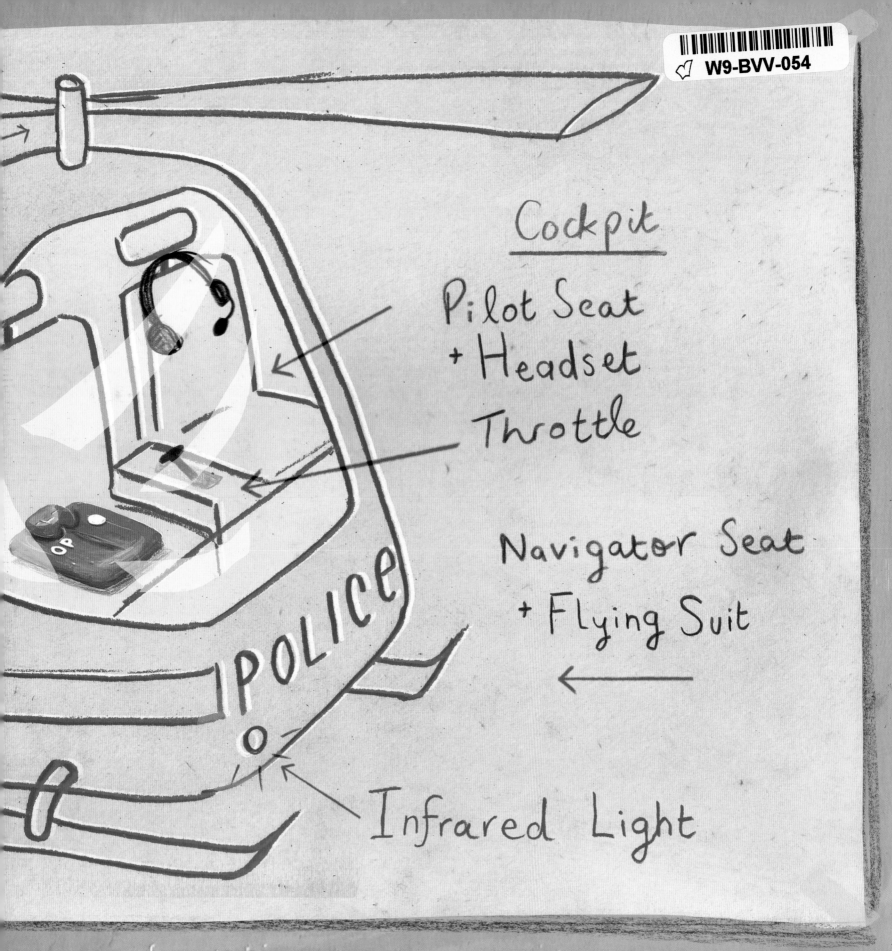

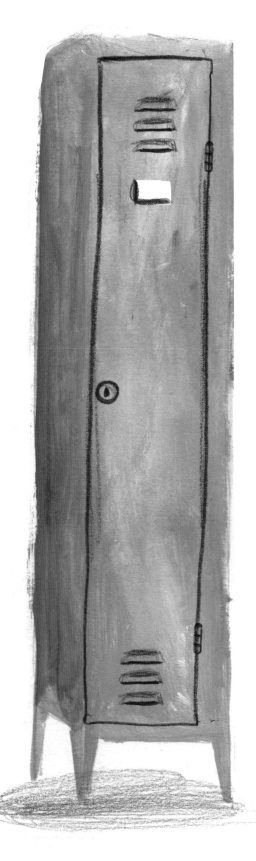

# TO NAN YORKE, 1929-2015

Officer Panda: Sky Detective
Copyright © 2016 by Ashley Crowley

ISBN 978-0-06-236627-6

The artist used mixed media, including pencils, colored pencils, inks, gouache paint, and graphite sticks, and Adobe Photoshop to create the illustrations for this book.

Design by Chelsea C. Donaldson
16 17 18 19 20  SCP  10 9 8 7 6 5 4 3 2 1
❖
First Edition

# Officer Panda
## Sky Detective

BY

ASHLEY CROWLEY

HARPER
An Imprint of HarperCollinsPublishers

# 9:30 A.M.: BAG IS SEALED.

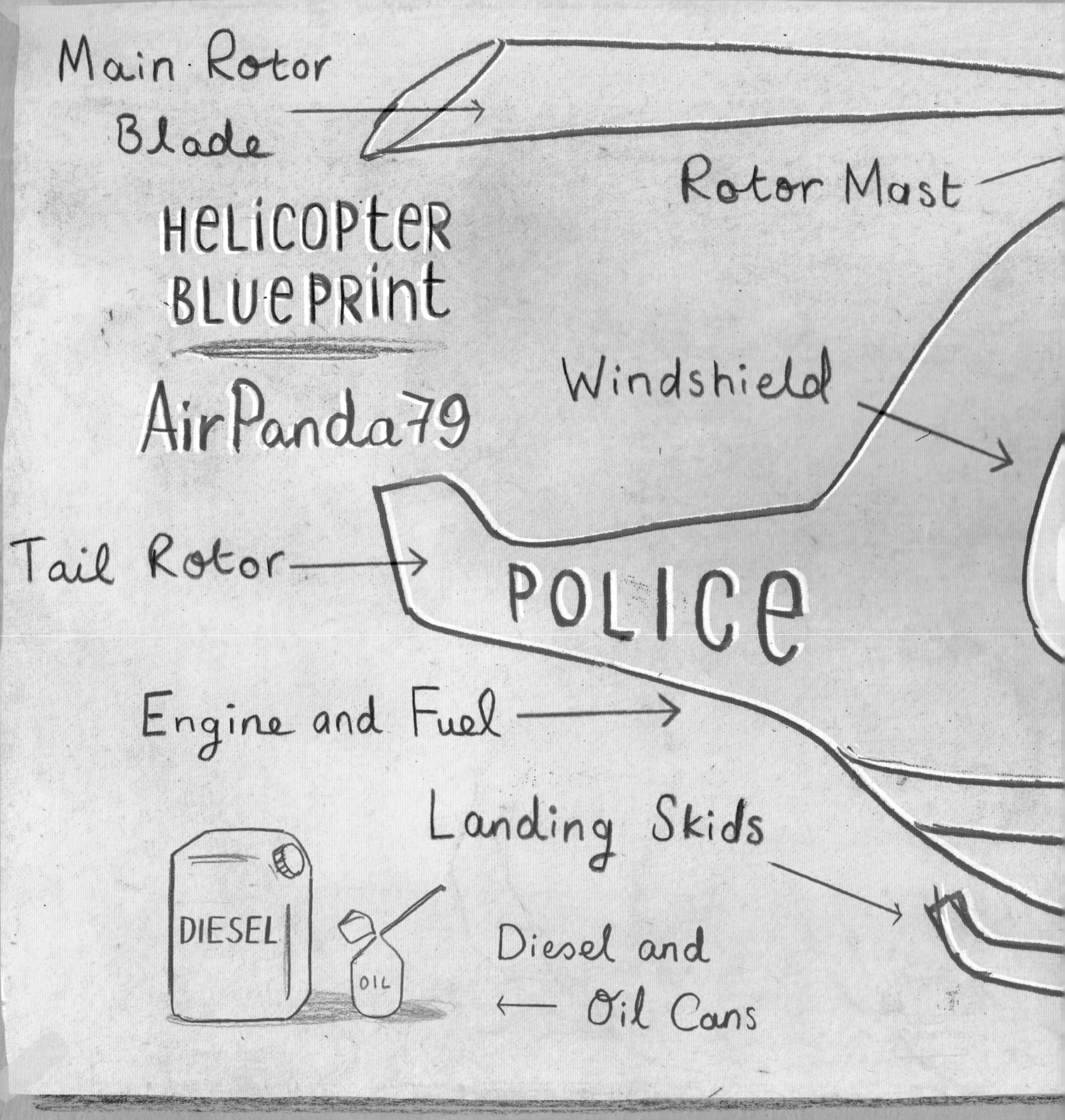

Main Rotor
Blade

Rotor Mast

# HELICOPTER
# BLUEPRINT

Windshield

AirPanda79

Tail Rotor

POLICE

Engine and Fuel

Landing Skids

DIESEL

OIL

Diesel and
← Oil Cans